EverMourne

WESLEY EAGLE

First, I swore she was still there..a whisper in the walls..a shadow in the doorframe. Denial is a cruel, beautiful thing.

Then, I cursed the river, the sky, the gods, myself. I howled at the moon, but the night did not answer.

I bartered with ghosts, offered my breath for hers. But the dead make no deals, and silence was my only reply.

Then, the weight came. A quiet, endless drowning. Grief is not fire. It is water. Slow. Inevitable. Deep.

And finally, I stood in the storm, and let the sky weep with me. I did not run. I did not kneel. I only walked forward.

— Unknown

To those who have lost, to those
who will, and to the ones we
carry with us still.

THE WOMAN

She carried her daughter with her, always.

Not in her arms, nor in laughter filling the home, but in the silence. In the dust that thickened on untouched shelves. In the way the wooden floor creaked beneath her rough, bare feet, as if the house itself sighed with her.

The morning light, soft and golden, stretched through the shutters, cutting across the small, cluttered space. It illuminated the cups left unwashed, and the table littered with forgotten things. A half-burned candle sat crooked in its holder, ready to fall. A small chair, once tucked neatly under the table, was slightly askew, as if someone had just been sitting there.

She did not tidy.

She had stopped trying.

Instead, she moved toward the small hearth, where the iron kettle sat in its usual place. She reached for the familiar bundle of dried flowers and blueberry juice. What was left of the butterfly pea blossoms left a deep blue against her fingertips. Her hands trembled as she measured them into the cup, watching as the water darkened, swirling into the color her daughter had loved so much.

"Like magic!" she had once giggled, cupping her small hands around the warm ceramic.

The magic in this home was gone now.

The memory sat beside the woman as she sipped in silence.

She did not cry. Not anymore.

Instead, she let the tea settle in her chest, warm, but not comforting.

It no longer was.

She sat in stillness as the world outside woke without her.

Beyond the window, crows cawed from the trees. Their cries cut through the morning air, slicing the cold with their grating sound.

The wind stirred through the open shutters, carrying the scent of morning bread from the village beyond. She heard the distant, rhythmic clang of a blacksmith at his forge. The world moved on without her.

It always had.

Even before the incident, she had been on the edges of their world. The husbandless woman. The woman whose child had no father. The woman who lived alone in the small, forgotten dwelling at the village's edge.

They had never said it outright, not when she first arrived, not when her daughter was born, not in the years she spent scraping by with quiet resilience. But she had always felt it. The sideways glances, the whispers that lingered just beneath the surface of conversation. A woman on her own was something unnatural. Something to be pitied at best, distrusted at worst.

And now, she had given them a reason to confirm what they already suspected. A reason to call her cursed.

Her tired eyes drifted, almost unthinking, across the room.

Near the door, a small pair of shoes still sat neatly side by side. Untouched. A thin film of dust dulled their once white color, as though time had tried to claim them, but had not quite succeeded.

In the farthest corner of the room, a

stuffed rabbit lay slumped against the wall, its fur tangled with cobwebs. Its stitched mouth still curved in a quiet, patient smile. Waiting for its playmate to return.

Above the hearth, a picture of her daughter, her face caught mid-laugh, had fallen from its frame.

Tucked against the wall, near the back door, a folded quilt in a box lay defeated where she had placed it. Forgotten, dust settling into the folds of its once vibrant fabric.

By the window, a line of small clothes hung limp, still damp with sorrow. Left out to dry but never removed. The clothing had stiffened, the scent of river water long faded, but she forgot. She had meant to take them down.

But she never did.

Her fingers curled around the rim of the empty cup.

She had been inside too long. The thought was sudden. Unwelcome.

Her fingers tightened around the hot ceramic, debating. But in the end, she rose. She would go to the village today. It was not a grand decision. Not a meaningful one, but it was movement.

She turned, stepping past the forgotten shoes, the small fallen portrait, the cobwebbed rabbit, the dusty blanket, the clothes still waiting to be folded . . . all the things she had let time settle over.

For the first time in three weeks, she reached for her cloak.

After taking a long, deep breath, she

opened her door.

And she stepped outside.

The village had not changed. It still hummed with life, just as it had before.

Market stalls lined the cobbled square, their canopies fluttering in the wind. The air was ripe with the scent of fresh bread, roasting chestnuts, and something spiced drifting from the apothecary's door. Children wove through the crowd, their laughter ringing like bells. Merchants called out their wares. Coins clinked. Sly voices bartered dubious wares. Life went on, as if nothing happened.

As if *she* never happened.

The woman moved through it unseen. No one turned to look at her, not at first. But she felt them . . . the glances, the quiet pauses in conversation, the murmurs just beneath the surface.

They knew who she was. They knew what had happened. And they judged her for it.

She gripped the handle of her basket tighter, holding her breath as if that would help her disappear.

She kept her green eyes down, weaving past carts of ripened pears, dried meats, and sugared almonds. She did not stop until she reached the small shop tucked at the edge of the square.

The bell chimed softly as she entered

inside the old, dusty shop.

Warmth wrapped all around her. The familiar scent of dried herbs, parchment, and lavender oil. This place had always been a quiet, safe place. A place she had once brought her sweet daughter, the child's small hands brushing along the shelves, her voice full of endless questions.

Other patrons mingled and murmured in hushed voices as she entered.

The shopkeeper beamed happily at her from behind the counter.

"Oh my! It's been quite a while since I've seen you here!"

She only nodded.

The woman stepped around a crate of dried sage, brushing flour from her apron. "What can I get you, dear?"

"Lavender," she murmured. "And sugar cane."

The shopkeeper clasped her hands together. "Oh, that's right! You always got those with . . ."

Silence.

A breath held in the air, fragile and unspoken. The color drained from the woman's face immediately. Her mouth hung open as if the words had just now caught up to her.

The shopkeeper had forgotten.

Just for a second.

The world was already forgetting her. How could it?

She had spoken as though nothing had changed, as though there was still a small girl waiting at home to bake her favorite treat.

But there wasn't.

The shopkeeper swallowed hard.

"I-I . . ." she faltered, her hands twisting in the fabric of her apron. "I'm so sorry. I didn't mean to . . . I—"

"It's fine," the woman said.

Her voice was flat. Empty. Tired.

The shopkeeper hurried to the shelves, pulling down bundles of dried lavender and a small wrapped block of sugar cane. She set them on the counter with careful hands.

"No charge," she said quickly.

The woman left the coins anyway. She gathered the items into her basket, fingers brushing against the woven rim. The air in the shop felt constrictive and suffocating.

She needed to leave. Now.

As she turned toward the door, she heard them. The whispers.

She didn't have to look to know that the other women in the shop had stopped talking. That they were staring now, their voices hushed beneath the sound of clattering horses outside, and other patrons half-hearted conversations.

"She's still grieving."

"Poor thing. She hasn't been the same since."

"Did you hear? Someone said she still keeps the child's things just as they were."

"I heard she wasn't even there to stop it. She just let her wander off. Seems it could've been avoided."

"Terrible shame. Terrible mother."

She hung her basket of goods on her elbow and forced herself forward.

She would be home soon. Out of this wretched place. But then, a voice from behind a shelf spoke out. Soft and certain, like it knew.

"I heard she's going into Kyohi Forest."

She stilled.

"Don't be ridiculous," a man's voice muttered. "No one ever goes into that place. It is evil. It is filled with tricks. It is filled with death."

"But I heard she's looking for . . . the Witch."

The sentence settled heavy in the small shop air.

The Witch.

"Another fool goes to seek the Witch," a

man grumbled. "She won't return. None of them ever do."

"Aye," another voice agreed, quieter. "There was one before. Years ago. Never seen again. Either she found what she sought . . . or died trying."

She kept walking, pushing through the door, out into the cold, open air. The bell jingling loudly from her rushed exit, as a murder of crows stared down from the rooftop.

The black creatures cawed after her, mirroring the surrounding gossip as she strode off.

She did not stop until the village was behind her.

Back at her home, the scent of lavender filled the small, cold dwelling at the edge of the village.

It curled through the air, sweet and warm, weaving between the cracks in her plastered walls, settling into the dust that had made a home there. She had not baked in weeks.

Her kitchen felt different because of it.

The soft scrape of her spoon against the wooden bowl. The way the flour puffed into the air when she pressed her palms into the dough. The warmth rising from the oven, wrapping around her like a quiet embrace.

For a moment, just a small moment, it felt as if nothing had changed at all.

Her hands worked with a rhythm they had not forgotten. With a rhythm she had danced to every week for seven years.

Measure. Stir. Shape.

Seven years . . .

She had done this many times. Her daughter's small hands had once mirrored her own, rolling out dough beside her, giggling as flour dusted her tiny nose. Guiding those chubby fingers to twist the batter into shapes.

She closed her eyes.

Seven years . . .

She could almost hear it.

The laughter in the room, the small humming of her child's voice, the consuming of fresh, lavender cookies. The past and present blurring for a fleeting second, until . . . the oven crackled.

The moment was gone.

She inhaled sharply and set the spoon aside on the counter. She moved methodically, laying the small lavender cookies onto a tray, pressing each one gently with a single heart shape before sliding them into the fire-warmed oven.

She watched them bake, sitting silently in the small chair her daughter once occupied.

By the time the cookies cooled, the sky outside had deepened to the color of twilight ink.

She sat at the table, the basket before her.

She had waited long enough.

The rumors had been whispered all her life. Before she was even born it seemed.

The Witch of Kyohi Forest was nothing more than a story told in hushed voices, a warning passed like rumor in the market square. A woman who could do the impossible. A powerful woman who could take away pain. Who had the power to do the unimaginable.

Some said she would kill you and eat

you.

Some said she would simply take what you carried, leaving your arms empty and heart hollow.

Some said she could bring the dead back to the realm of the living.

No one agreed on the truth. But no one dared to find out. The forest was dangerous. The forest was alive. No one who entered came back the same. If they ever came back at all.

And yet . . .

There were rules.

The stories, despite their contradictions, always spoke of the same thing: if you sought the Witch's power, you had to bring her something of the one you lost.

Not just anything. The four best things.

The objects most tied to their essence.

The things that held pieces of them, soaked with their presence, their touch, their joy.

The spell could not work without them.

So, she had chosen carefully.

Meticulously.

Her eyes welled as she reached for the first item.

The small, painted picture.

She turned it over carefully, as though the movement itself might disturb the girl smiling within its edges. The frame was cracked from when it had fallen, so she'd discarded it. The portrait was all she needed anyway.

Next, the small bundle of lavender cookies, carefully wrapped in cloth. The smell was still strong. Sweet, but no longer warm. Her daughter's favorite.

She hesitated on the stuffed rabbit.

Its fur, once soft, was tangled from years

of being held. Her daughter had clutched it every night. It felt wrong somehow, to take it. Bringing it to her face she could still smell her. Oh how she missed that smell. Yet, she placed it in the basket anyway.

The quilt was last.

It was old, worn from years of use, its once-vibrant threads faded with time. A patchwork of fabric scraps, stitched together with love.

Her daughter had adored it.

On extra cold nights, they would burrow beneath it together, the warmth of their bodies melting into its softness. It had been a fortress in the living room, draped over chairs to make castles. A ship on stormy seas. A hiding place from monsters, always made safe again by the glow of a candle and a mother's arms.

The rabbit had always been part of the

stories.

Her daughter would press its little paws together, whispering funny secrets only the stuffed creature could hear, wrapping it snugly in the blanket before curling up beside it for her afternoon naps.

Gingerly, the woman folded it, and tucked it delicately into the basket beside the rest.

Tightening her cloak around her shoulders, she pulled the basket close and stepped toward the door.

It was night now. Only the moon illuminated the land. But the moon was all she needed.

The house was dark behind her, weighted with things left unsaid. With life not lived.

She did not look back. She stepped over the threshold, and she left.

The field stretched before her, golden and brittle beneath the moonlight.

The brisk wind moved through it in slow, whispering waves, bending the stalks of dried grass like a thousand reaching hooks. They brushed against her legs as she walked, clawing and snagging at the hem of her cloak, as if trying to slow her. As if trying to stop her.

She did not stop.

Kyohi forest loomed ahead, black against the dark sky. An endless wall of trees, their branches tangled so thickly that not even the moonlight could reach beyond their might.

She reached the edge and halted.

The difference was instant.

The air was still here. The wind that had followed her through the field died at the tree line. The world beyond the forest felt deeper, vaster, as though it had no end.

She let out a slow breath and watched as the wisps of grey exited her mouth.

Then, she lowered the basket to the ground.

Her fingers clenched around the fabric of her cloak, pulling it tighter around herself, as if the existence of it could anchor her. She was not afraid. Not truly. But something in the forest watched and waited. She could feel it.

For a moment, she turned.

The village beyond still burned soft and warm in the distance. The light from the windows flickered like small, golden lanterns against the dark.

The woman thought of all the whispers.

"She's still grieving."

"Poor thing, she hasn't been the same."

"Did you hear? It was her fault."
The woman swallowed. Then she huffed. She bent, lifted the basket back into her arms, and without another glance at the village, marched forward. That's when the forest swallowed her whole.

THE FOREST

It was ever so dark.

Not the kind of darkness that one's eyes could ever adjust to, but something deeper. Something that stretched in all directions, soaking into the spaces between the trees, thick as parchment ink.

She followed the path that lay before her, though it was little more than a narrow strip of ground where nothing grew. It twisted between the trunks, winding deeper and deeper into the unseen abyss.

Her steps slowed, and the silence all around pressed in upon her ears.

The wind had not followed her. The crickets, the distant hoot of an owl, the rustling of small creatures in the grass . . . none of it had come inside this place. The only sound was her breathing.

That is, until she heard a voice. Small at first, but unmistakable. Soft. Familiar. Sweet. Perfect.

"Mommy?"

She stopped in her tracks.

It was ahead of her, just beyond the path, somewhere behind the trees. Her breath ceased. Her body became rigid as an arrow.

Then, slowly . . . ever so slowly, she turned her head.

And there she was.

Small. Barefoot. Her pink nightdress slightly wrinkled, as if she had just climbed out of bed. Hair wild, eyes sleepy and confused.

Her daughter.

She blinked up at her, rubbing at one eye with the back of her hand.

"Mommy?" she said again. "What are you doing in the forest?"

Her daughter stood there, small and real and whole, as if nothing had ever happened.

As if the days had not passed.

As if the river had not taken her.

As if the grave she had stood over did not exist.

The girl tilted her head, blinking up at her with soft confusion. The same eyes, the same voice. The same little hands that had once reached for her in the night.

"What are you doing here?" her daughter asked again, her voice light in questioning, as if nothing was wrong.

It was real. This was real. It had to be real.

Her lips parted, but no words came.

The child took a small step closer.

"Come on, Mommy," she said, reaching out. "Let's go home. I'm tired."

Home.

It was such a simple word.

Her feet moved before she realized what

she was doing. A step forward. Then another.

The trees around her seemed to open, shifting with the movement, clearing the path back the way she had come. Leading her back.

She should not be here.

Her daughter was alive. She had always been alive.

What was she doing in this forest then? What was she looking for? Why was her basket full of these things?

She did not know. It did not matter.

Her daughter's hand was warm in hers, small fingers curling into her palm like they always had. A shape so familiar, she could have held it with her eyes closed and known it as surely as she knew her own name.

And so she walked, back through the trees. Back through the quiet. Back to the edge of the forest.

And as they stepped out into the field of the tall, dry grass, it all came crashing back.

The memories slammed into her like a rush of icy water, sudden and merciless. The weight, the sorrow, the reason she had come. The child's small hand was suddenly gone. She turned, but there was nothing. Only the empty, swaying field. Only the trees, dark and watching. Mocking her.

Her knees nearly buckled beneath her. The forest had taken her daughter from her again.

Denying her. Denying her the truth.

No.

She straightened, wiping at her face with the back of her sleeve. She turned on her heel and stepped back into the trees.

It happened the same way. A voice, calling. A little girl, blinking up at her.

"Mommy? What are you doing in the forest?"

The mother blinked, confusion flooding her once more. Had she come to get her? Had the child wandered out of bed and gotten lost? She must have.

Yes.

That was it.

She sighed, relieved, bending to pick her up. The child curled against her shoulder, warm and sleepy. She carried her toward home. She stepped out of the forest . . . and her arms were empty.

The mother let out a sharp, gasping breath. She stumbled, her hands trembling as they clutched at the basket in her other hand.

The child was gone. Again. Her body still ached with the phantom weight of her.

The forest had tricked her twice. It would not happen again.

The woman pressed a hand to her chest, trying to still the trembling inside her. For a long moment, she stood in the field, staring at the dark tree line before her.

The village was behind her, the forest ahead.

She had left the village willingly. She had chosen this path. And yet, standing here, her body ached to turn back. To walk home. To lie down and let herself sink into the quiet. She did not.

Instead, she reached into the basket and grasped the small portrait.

Its edges were rough against her fingers, worn from time, from being held, from being carried like a talisman. Gripping it tightly, she flinched. A sharp, thin sting bit into her fingertip. She looked down, startled. A small bead of crimson welled at the edge of her thumb, bright against the paper's faded corner. The sight grounded her.

She brought her hand close, pressing her lips to the wound, the metallic tang of blood touching her tongue.

Real.

This was real.

Nothing could deny that. Not even this

forest.

She exhaled. Let the pain steady her.

She would remember.

She would not forget.

She turned and walked back inside. The darkness closed around her, but she did not falter. The forest knew. She had seen through its lies. She had walked through its tricks, held them in her hands, carried them to the edge and let them dissolve into nothing. She would not be fooled again.

So, the forest changed.

It would have to try something else. Something she could not hold. Something she could not touch or carry. Something that would slip through her fingers, through her mind, before she even realized she had lost it.

The trees now whispered. Not in words, not this time. Oh no, they would sing.

A melody.

It drifted through the branches, soft and distant. A lullaby carried on the wind.

The mother stopped walking. She knew that song. Her daughter's song.

The tune was faint, just on the edge of hearing, as if it had been there all along. A thread woven into the forest itself, waiting to be pulled.

She turned her head, listening. The sound came from somewhere deeper. Beyond the path.

She should not follow it. She knew that.

Regardless of that knowledge, her feet moved, slow and careful, her fingers curling tighter around the picture, taking one step off the trail.

Then another.

The path behind her faded into the dark, swallowed by the trees, but she didn't turn back.

The lullaby swelled, weaving through the air like a ribbon, curling through the leaves, calling her forward. Calling her away from the path.

She moved toward it, past the odd shaped plants, the scurrying rodents, and a beautiful clearing bathed in violet light.

Butterflies.

Hundreds of them, flickering like embers in the dark. Their wings pulsed with soft, purple light. She had never seen butterflies like this before.

Beautiful.

The lullaby continued to hum all around her.

The butterflies flickered again in response to the sound, breaking apart and scattering into the dark. The song wavered. The lullaby was no longer a lullaby.

It was something else. Something thinner. Something . . . hollow. The song was now entirely gone, replaced by howling. Loud, sudden, and violent howling.

The branches above her rattled, bending as if the unexpected wind had large hands, as if it could reach down and tear her from the earth.

With all the commotion around her, something ripped. Not fabric. Something worse. Way worse.

Paper.

Her fingers snapped open just in time to see the small portrait caught in the wind, twisting and spiraling higher.

"No!"

She lunged for it, but the storm had already stolen it away, carrying it higher, higher and higher until a branch snapped. Then a second branch. And then a third. The sound was deafening as the forest tore the portrait apart. The pieces scattered like lost feathers, swallowed by the wind.

Gone.

She stumbled back, chest heaving, hands empty. That had been the last picture of her daughter. The last thing she had.

Gone forever.

Her mouth opened wide, but no sobs

came. No sound at all. She only stood there, staring at the empty space where it had been. The wind howled louder, the forest screaming in triumph.

But she was silent. Her fingers balled into fists.

She still had the basket. She still had three things left, and she was still going to move forward.

Whether the forest agreed or not.

THE CROW

The forest felt different now after stealing her picture. Before, the woods had been clever and deceptive. Its illusions curled around her like silk, lulling her into a lie. Now, it seemed as if it was watching. Knowing.

The silence around her was too thick. Waiting. Expectant.

The path was gone. She had wandered too far and was entirely at the mercy of the trees. She had been so careful, she thought. She had walked straight ahead, she was sure of it. But nothing looked familiar.

She turned in slow circles, scanning around herself, searching for a landmark. Anything to reorient herself. Spinning in endless circles.

But the deeper she looked, the more everything bled together.

She let out a slow breath. "Stay calm," she whispered to herself.

She could not let herself panic. Not now. She glanced down at the basket in her hands. Three things left.

Three.

As she gazed upon her items, a

snapping twig caused her to gasp. A rustle. The caw of a crow.

She twirled around.

Another caw. Another snap of a twig.

This was not the wind or the leaves. This was something moving.

Watching.

"Are you lost, miss?"

She spun toward the voice so fast, she almost twisted an ankle.

A figure stood within the darkest shades of the trees. Small, cloaked, barely more than a shadow against the dark forest backdrop.

For a long moment, neither of them moved.

Then, the figure stepped forward, and what existed of the surrounding moonlight caught him.

A spirit. Or at least that was what she guessed. She had never seen one in person before.

He was small . . . not childlike, but not quite full-grown either. Standing no taller than her chest, with thin, wiry limbs wrapped in a tattered black cloak, his long black feathers spilled from beneath the hood. His eyes deep and dark. His mask was simple, red, and smooth. The sharp beak of it curving downward in an elegant point.

It almost made him look . . . kind.

Safe.

"You look quite tired miss," he mused, his voice light and pleasant. "And very far from home, I'm sure."

She did not answer. She was not sure if she should.

Still, he did not move closer. He only tilted his head the other way. His red eyes flickered downward.

The basket.

"Miss," he asked gently. "You have food, don't you? May I trouble you for just a morsel? I am ever so hungry."

The woman swallowed. She had given up so much already.

But . . . he had not asked for much. Just a small piece wouldn't hurt.

She hesitated, then slowly knelt, reaching into the basket. She broke off a piece of one of the cookies and held it out in her palm. Like feeding a horse.

The crow spirit tilted his head again.

With a slow, deliberate movement, he lifted a feathered hand and slid the mask away. His true face was beneath.

It was not smooth. Not soft. But sharp, black, and real.

His beak was sleek and hooked, his dark eyes reflected fire like two pinpricks of red ember.

"I am Ikari. And I am ever so grateful for you, miss."

The woman nodded, staring at this strange creature. This spirit in front of her. He felt . . . familiar.

Ikari's feathers ruffled slightly, and he let out a small click. His narrow, feathered arm flexed as he reached for the cookie. His thin and lanky fingered hand emerged from his cloak. Almost human.

The dark plumes along his knuckles rumpled as his fingers wrapped around the offering.

For a moment, he simply stood there, eating, his talons just barely visible beneath the feathers of his hand, like mutated fingernails.

Then, he smiled.

"You are kind."

His voice was soft and sincere.

She exhaled slowly. This spirit was safe. Something she desperately needed.

He gestured toward the dark.

"This forest is a confusing place," he spoke. "But I know every single path. I could lead you back on your way, if you so desire?"

She hesitated before nodding. Safe and

helpful? Perhaps this journey would be an easy one.

The crow spirit turned, and she followed. And together, in the darkness, they walked.

The forest stretched long and endlessly ahead of them, but at least now she was not alone. Ikari walked beside her, his black cloak swaying with every step. His bare feet made no sound against the damp earth.

He was very polite. Chatty, at times even. He spoke of the forest as if it were an old friend. One with moods, with tempers, with secrets it did not easily share. He spoke of his friends, and some spirits he did not get along with. He rambled it all. And she listened.

"This forest does not like to let go of those who wander too far in," he said at one point, glancing at her. "Not unless it wants to."

The path he led her down did not feel like a path at all. There were no markers, no signs of anything but the same gnarled trees, as if they were walking in circles. Still, she continued to follow him. She did not have a choice in the matter. She was a stranger to these woods.

Ikari glanced sideways at her, as if he could sense her thoughts. "You know," he murmured, "not many travelers make it through here this far."

The woman said nothing.

"You must be very strong," he continued, his voice light, pleasant. "Very clever."

He smiled again. Not a wide smile, not forced. Just the kind of small, simple smile that made her feel that perhaps she could trust him with anything. She had made a friend.

Out of nowhere, he stopped walking. His beak closed. But she could hear his heavy breathing through the holes that sat atop it. Ikari's eyes once again focused toward the basket.

"You must be hungry," he said.

She was. Her body was weak with exhaustion, her limbs aching with the weight of the walking they had endured.

How long had it been? She did not know.

He hummed. "You have food still, don't you?"

"Yes."

"May I bother you for another bite, miss? Walking has made me quite peckish."

She had already given him one. And yet . . . She sighed. He had helped her come this far. What would be the harm? She reached into the basket, breaking off a small piece of another cookie.

Ikari's fingers quivered. He took it from her, slower this time. His feathered hand brushed against hers, clenching into a fist as he brought it back to himself. His hand had been burning hot. Too smooth for something that should have been flesh. It was an odd feeling.

The moment he had the cookie, he bit into it with quiet satisfaction. But, as his beaked opened and closed, it snapped in a way it hadn't before. With a force that was rough. Destructive.

"You are very kind," he murmured between chews. But something didn't sit right, now. There was something else between those words. Something off. Something cruel. Something angry. Almost like muted fury, held back between every chomp he made.

The woman said nothing. She just wanted to get to the path. Something else stirred within Ikari, and the woman did not like it.

The quicker they reached the path, the better.

It had been hours since they had started their walk and it was beginning to get cold, so the woman decided to make a small camp.

After finding a quiet spot to stop, the woman decided to build a fire. She sat on the ground, her basket beside her, her hands curled into her lap as the firelight licked the dark air. The stuffed rabbit sat beside her as she pulled the quilt around her shoulders, shivering from a small gust of wind that broke through the air.

Ikari sat across from her. Still. Silent

now. Festering.

He had not touched his mask since the first time he removed it, and it hung loosely from a strap around his waist. His true face had remained visible, his black feathers gleaming in the dim glow. No matter where she turned to ignore the awkwardness, it seemed as if his piercing eyes were fixated on her, silently screaming through to her soul.

She tried not to look at him too much. Instead, she focused on the flames in front of her. The warmth was weak but enough. She was so tired now. The night had felt endless. The warmth did not help her exhaustion, and she felt as if maybe dozing off would be best. But a part of her didn't want to sleep.

Not with him here.

Ikari shifted slightly. He had not blinked in some time. The fire reflected off his already red eyes. Despite the bright glow of the fire, his pupils had a surging darkness to them.

His voice broke the silence.

"I am ever so hungry."

She exhaled. She had only a few cookies left, and she needed them.

"May I have another cookie, miss?" His words seemed kind. But they were laced with something new, almost venomous. Perhaps her tiredness was getting the best of her. He had been nothing but helpful.

He was still watching her. Still smiling. But now, that smile made her feel uneasy.

"Give me another cookie," he snapped.

She reached into the basket and handed him a cookie reluctantly. Only three cookies remained.

Ikari snatched it.

And then, before she could even realize what had happened, he took them all. Grabbing the basket from her hands in the swiftest of motions.

She gasped.

Her hands shot forward instinctually, tugging at the basket as if she could pull them back from him.

But it was already done.

The last crumbs fell from his pointed fingers, as he licked the edge of his beak. His red eyes glowing like embers in the dark. He was successful in his consumption.

The woman stared at him. Her stomach twisted, grief and rage curling in her throat like bile.

She now only had two items left.

"How . . ." Her voice was a breathy gasp. "How could you?"

Ikari's feathers ruffled smugly. He tilted his head, his expression carefully neutral.

"I was hungry, miss."

"They were all I had left," she said, voice breaking. "Why?"

She was shaking. Her fury rose like a tide at the mercy of a full moon.

He did not care.

"WHY?" She screamed.

As he looked at her, his body began to stretch, ever so subtly.

The shadows behind him moved in

unison, but not from the flicker of fire between them.

"You owed me," he snarled. His voice was different now. Deeper. Guttural. Crow-like.

"For being your guide."

His smile widened. It did not stop widening.

"But you see," he yelled, "I am still so hungry. Ever so hungry!"

The fire flickered.

And the rage around him swirled. The heat she felt no longer emanated from just the fire, but now from his body.

A gust of wind cut through the trees, making the embers swirl, red against the dark, sparkling in his crimson, glossy eyes.

Ikari was changing. His form stretched.

The cloak that once draped around him was now barely able to contain the shape beneath. His limbs grew longer, his fingers stretching, curling into something sharp and predatory. The feathers along his hands bristled, shifting, darkening as they thickened into larger, razor sharp wings.

The ground hissed beneath his feet, the dirt blackening as if scorched by something deep, burning, and unseen. Something from the pits of hell itself.

And his face.

His sharp beak widened.

It did not stop.

It split open. The soft edges of his hooked mouth tore too far down, extending into something gaping, monstrous, and unhinged.

Teeth. Rows upon rows of them, lining the cavernous abyss of his mouth. His throat glowed from within, a deep, churning red like a fire from a dragon. The ember-light of hunger. Of rage. Of pure, unfiltered hatred. Pure, seething anger.

And yet, the worst part was not how he looked.

It was that he was still smiling.

The woman stumbled backward.

Her hands clutched at the empty basket like a shield, as if somehow it could protect her from what was growing in front of her.

Ikari then took a step forward, over the fire.

And another.

The fire shrunk against the wind, as if it too was trying to retreat from the horror that was unfolding.

She could not breathe.

He towered over her, his black wings stretching outward, bellowing into the night like smoke. He exhaled, and the sound was not a breath, but a rattling growl. A sound that carried the weight of something bottomless. Something primal. Something starving.

"You gave me so much already, miss," he cawed furiously.

His voice was wrong. It was distorted and muffled, like words through water. The red glow of his throat pulsed as he spoke.

"But it is not enough."

She completely recognized this spirit.

This embodiment.

He was there to take her.

To envelop her.

The woman scrambled backwards, forcing herself to stand while her eyes remained locked on the spirit.

"I want more. I want YOU!"

And then he lunged. Without hesitating, she ran.

The basket dropped from her arms as she spun, her bare feet digging into the dirt, kicking up dust as she tore through the trees. Branches lashed at her arms, cutting her face, but she didn't care.

She had to escape.

Behind her, she could hear it. The sound of something too large moving too fast.

Ikari.

The ground trembled beneath the weight of it. His wings dragged against the trees, snapping branches, sending leaves cascading in a flurry of black and red.

He was faster than her.

He was closer than he should have been.

Something hot and damp curled around her ankle, stinging her flesh. She screamed, kicking, thrashing, desperate to pull away.

His tongue. It had wrapped around her

like a vine, dragging her backward for just a split second. Her leg burned as she fought against the pull, fought against the endless, cavernous hunger behind her. The forest shook with his rage as Ikari thundered after her.

The night pulsed with his voice. Layered and deep. A thousand furious voices inside one gigantic monster.

"I want all of you!!"

All she could do was run. That was all she had against this beast. This monstrosity of hate. This anger that resonated against every inch of her skin.

And she was scared. He would consume her. Take all of her.

But he was gaining. She could feel the hot air shift as his massive body came closer. She could only run forward.

Suddenly, the trees broke open and the ground almost disappeared. She skidded to a halt, her bare feet sliding in the loose dirt, rocks tumbling down into water below with a cacophony of splashes.

A river.

The water was deep, dark, and fast. The surface rippled in silvery streaks beneath the moonlight, black and endless, curling over itself in slow, steady currents. The sound of it crashing and roaring against the rocks began to make her dizzy. The sight of it sent a ringing in her ears as memories cracked against her mind like thunder.

Water in her lungs.

The weight of a small body in her arms.

A scream swallowed by the current.

Fingers slipping from her grasp.

She gasped, choking on her own breath, stepping back.

The growl rumbled behind her still. Hot, slow, like an animal coiling to strike.

He was right behind her now. Hungry. Ready to consume her.

She turned.

Ikari had stopped. Smiling at his prey, knowing she was trapped.

His wings dragged against the dirt, his mouth stretched open too wide, still grinning, still snarling. His red eyes burned through her, locking her in place. Liquid fire dripped from his open mouth. She was trapped.

The river at her back.

The beast before her.

Ikari's clawed fingers flexed, ready for his meal. His voice came slow, sharp, almost teasing.

"You let her go," he snarled. "YOU LET HER GO, and you did NOTHING! Just like you're doing now."

Another step.

"Watched her slip away."

Her breath became short, rapid. He was right.

"And now, you're running again."

The woman looked down at the raging river behind her again. The merciless, cruel, vile river below.

"But now, there is nowhere left to run, miss."

She could feel the pull of the water behind her. The heat of his breath before her. The past and the present colliding, crushing her between them.

Her eyes slid shut.

She took a slow, steady breath. And then, she turned.

Not to run. Not to fight.

But to face him.

His breath seared the air between them, carrying the scent of burnt embers and something deeper, something rotting, decayed, like a fire that had long since died but still smoldered beneath the ash. His mouth, his terrible, gaping mouth, stretched open wider, wider, red teeth gleaming in the dark. She could see herself reflected in the hollow pits of his amber eyes.

Compared to him, she was small. Weak.

Afraid.

She stepped forward.

Then he lunged.

She met him before he could strike. She threw her arms around him, squeezing her eyes shut as she did so.

And held him.

The impact knocked the breath from her lungs. His large, distorted body was sharp and wrong. The jerky movements from his endless wings were like holding onto a searing tornado. His feathers burned like cinders beneath her hands. His sharp claws dug into her back, causing her to bleed.

She screamed from the agonizing pain, but her hold remained locked.

Then, he screamed.

It was not a roar. Not a screech. It was a

wail.

A terrible, keening sound that split the night in two.

He thrashed in her arms. Ripping. Tearing. He tried to push her away. The anger he exuded was as powerful as her own. She felt it. Welling from within her, but also from this spirit. This angry, furious, terrible spirit.

She did not let go.

She held tighter.

His claws raked her skin. His beak snapped dangerously close to her face. His tormenting heat bore into her chest.

"Let me go!" he snarled.

She did not.

He wrung, convulsed, twisted violently, as if trying to tear himself from existence.

"LET ME GO!"

His body cracked at the edges with a dark, red light. His wings folded inward, the sound of burning flesh and crackling fire. His throat dimmed. His claws dulled.

He cooled.

The monstrous wail became something else.

Something smaller. Something . . . weaker.

"Please," he whispered.

His body was now warm. Like a sunny day.

The woman did not move. She felt him shrinking. Felt his form collapsing, folding, trembling within her arms. She lowered to her knees, cradling him.

He was cold now.

The wind howled.

The river rushed.

The writhing mass in her arms vanished, and in replacement was the flutter of small wings. A single black feather drifted through the air, before she had time to collect her thoughts.

She watched as it swayed, caught in the cold breeze, spiraling gently downward. She reached out, hand outstretched.

It landed softly in her palm, glowing for just a moment.

She curled her fingers around it, feeling the softness it contained. How beautiful it was.

She exhaled, looking up as the sound of a single caw cut through the roar of the water behind her. The unmistakable silhouette of a crow cut through the night sky, small and dark. Its body barely visible against the pale glow of the moon.

It circled once.

Then it was gone.

THE FOX

It had been hours since her encounter with Ikari. After returning to camp to retrieve her things, she did not remain to recoup. Instead, she trekked forward.

The path had felt endless. The trees, once thick and claustrophobic, had begun to thin. Their towering shapes no longer pressed so tightly together as she walked forward. A mountain loomed in the distance.

She swallowed hard, her throat raw, the air thick with the scent of damp earth and something bitter . . . the remnants of Ikari's rage still clinging to the trees.

Her legs felt very weak, unsteady, as she pressed a hand to the rough bark beside her, re-focusing herself.

She was still here. She had survived.

But had she won? She looked down at her basket of two. Her mind throbbing and ears ringing.

That ringing.

The sound in her ears would not leave her. Sounds that should not be.

They started faint at first, then stronger. A jingle of chains. The creak of wood.

A smell, too, carried on the still air . . . sweet, spiced, unnatural.

Her exhaustion was playing tricks on her. She needed to find the Witch.

The darkness of night was quickly fading. The black sky had softened at its edges, blurring into muted oranges. Slowly, the first hints of dawn pressed through the sky.

She kept walking. She had not stopped. Not when the wind had stolen the photograph from her grasp.

Not when she had run through the trees, fleeing the claws of a monster.

She had not stopped when the anger had nearly consumed her.

And she would not stop now.

The basket's weight pulled at her arm,

though it carried far less than before.

The cookies were gone. The photograph was dust.

Only two items remained.

A worn, stuffed rabbit and a quilted blanket.

She exhaled. Two items. Her steps slowed.

Was it enough? A flicker of doubt curled in her gut. She had not considered it before. Not until now. Not until she was here, lost in the heart of the woods, clutching what little remained of her daughter.

The stories had said the Witch needed four items. Four pieces of the departed's essence. But surely . . . surely if she was powerful enough to bring back the dead, she could make an exception. What was a rabbit and a quilt to someone who could bend the laws of nature?

The thought should have comforted her.

It did not.

She swallowed, throat now very dry. She hadn't drank water or eaten since she had left the village.

Her delicate fingers curled tighter around the basket handle, as if to anchor herself to something, anything, in the midst of the creeping doubt.

It will be enough.

It had to be enough.

She pressed forward, the morning light now bleeding through the trees. For the first time, the path ahead felt uncertain.

She had been so sure when she started. So certain that if she just followed the whispers, followed the stories, followed the path she would find what she needed.

But now? Now, everything felt farther away. What if she reached the Witch and found . . . nothing?

No answers. No magic. No daughter.

She bit her lip and shook the thought away. She hadn't realized before how much the forest had thinned as the sun rose. The darkness was giving way to something else.

One path coiled around the mountainside ahead, a narrow, treacherous trail where birds flew through jagged stone, whispering warnings only the foolish ignored. The ground there looked unstable. It was cracked and crumbling, as if daring her to trust it.

The other path plunged deeper into the woods, swallowed by jagged roots and darkened trees, pressed so tightly together, one would have to squeeze through to continue on.

Both seemed wrong.

She hesitated. Standing there, staring at the split in her path. Which way was the right way? Had she come all this way just to get lost? So many doubts had arisen in such a small period of time.

From behind her a sound called out, disrupting these thoughts.

A voice. A new voice.

Silky. Smooth. Smiling.

"Oh, dear traveler! What a terrible little predicament!"

She turned sharply. There, just off the

trail, sat a wagon. She had not heard it approach. Had not seen it. Had not sensed its presence until it wanted to be seen. It was just there.

It was large, wooden and worn, draped in tattered silks and jangling with chains and chimes. Small, broken lanterns swayed from its corners. Boxes and bags filled the bed and other things.

And atop it, a fox. No, not just a fox. A bearded, man-sized fox.

A beast in a purple traveler's robe, sat hunched and grinning, gold jewelry glinting against his dark, rust-colored fur. He was adorned with gold bracelets, bells, chains, and even an earring or two attached to his long, furry ears. His attire matched his cart, as if one set.

His long tail flicked lazily over the side of the cart, tapping against the wooden panels restlessly.

His bright, golden eyes gleamed down at her as he beamed smugly.

"Lost, are we dear?" He tsked.

"I'm . . . I'm looking for the Witch."

The Fox's ears flicked upward.

"Oh, the Witch," he hummed, moving his head in exaggerated thought. His large grin widened. His sharp teeth were hard not to stare at. Especially after her last encounter.

"Dear traveler, I know of *many* witches. What kind do you seek?"

He lifted a clawed, ringed finger.

"Left?" He pointed down one path.

"Right?" He gestured to the other.

He paused. Then smirked.

"Backward?"

She exhaled sharply. "The one who brings back the dead."

The woman was impatient.

The animal whistled. "Ahhh. That one." He tapped his furry, bearded chin. "Yes, yes . . . I may have heard of such a figure." His tail flicked. "But then again, perhaps she doesn't exist at all. Perhaps it is only a story, whispered by fools desperate for hope."

His beaming face hardened, sharp and glinting in the fresh morning sunlight as his tone became more serious. "Or perhaps . . . you simply haven't offered me enough incentive to remember."

The woman narrowed her eyes.

"Incentive?"

Taking note of her reaction, the fox swiftly hopped down from his cart.

"AHA! Where *ever* are my manners? Silly me. I am Pazari," he said, giving a low, exaggerated bow, "merchant of many things. Keeper of treasures both wanted and unwanted! The finest dealer in trades this side of the forest! And I absolutely *adore* a good bargain."

The woman kept her distance. She knew his kind. Foxes were never to be trusted. Especially in this place.

He scratched a claw against his scraggly beard again, surveying her. "Now, now, let me see . . . what could a woman like you possibly be searching for?"

"I do not have coin."

Pazari spread his arms, bright and theatrical at her flat response. "Oh that is quite alright, traveler! We are just here to chat! To mingle! And, to view my cart of wonders, yes?!" he declared. "You are clearly a woman of great taste. What do you seek? I have the finest silks, rich wines, rare jewels . . ."

His voice chimed happily as he reached behind him, pulling some small bags from his cart as he continued his spiel.

"Spices from distant lands, furs from the rarest of creatures, perfumes fit for queens, herbs that could make even the sourest of men fall in love with you! Everything!"

His eyes flicked to the basket in her arms. His sly, foxy grin reforming.

"Or perhaps . . . *something else.*" His

ring-adorned paw pointed toward the stuffed rabbit tucked carefully inside. "Toys . . . perhaps?"

The woman flinched, and Pazari's eyes sparkled.

"Aha." His voice was curled, smooth as the violet silk robe he wore.

"Now, that's interesting. Very, very interesting indeed."

The woman gritted her teeth. "I said. I have no coin," she spat.

Pazari gasped a dramatic, exaggerated noise.

"Oh, traveler! Oh whatever shall I do?!" He placed a furry hand over his heart, grabbing his chest as his face moved in closer. "Did you think I deal in something as dull as coin?"

He leaned closer to the woman, as if telling her a carefully guarded secret. His robe dragging against the dirt as he did so. He smelled of wet fur and musky perfume.

"I deal in *trade*," he whispered. "Bartering and bargaining only."

The woman turned her head away from the fox's face. His breath reeked of meat and honey. A terribly odd combination but pungent, nonetheless.

"I want nothing from you. Just to know which direction to travel," she stated flatly.

Pazari let out a long, exaggerated sigh, rolling his eyes so hard they nearly disappeared into the fluff of his face.

"Oh, but traveler, please. Indulge me. Humor a silly old fox."

The woman barely spared him a glance.

Her eyes drifted past him, past the chaotic array of boxes, cages, and crates stacked high upon his wagon. Some shuddered. Chains clinked. A faint, restless scratching stirred from within some cages.

She frowned at it all.

Rats. Birds. Cats. A mess of fur and feathers and restless, clawed things, all waiting to be released. And yet . . .

Her eyes were drawn upward at one of the cages. Just for a moment, it seemed . . . no. Couldn't be.

She looked away, her attention back to Pazari.

"There is nothing here that interests me," she repeated.

Pazari laughed a low, crackling sound that slithered beneath her skin. This fox felt slimy.

"Oh, but of *course*." He clapped his hands together, rings jangling like tiny bells. "A woman like you . . . so sharp, so refined, would not waste her time on such common filth."

His nose wrinkled as he waved a dismissive paw at the clutter around him, tail flicking as if disgusted by his own wares. Then, in an instant, his signature grin returned.

"No, no, no. Someone like you deserves so much more. Something rare. Something precious."

His voice softened, buttery smooth again.

"Something . . . *life-changing*."

The woman said nothing. Just looked

down at her basket. This was getting tiresome. She just wanted to leave.

Pazari's ears perked as if sensing something unsaid. Slowly, he leaned forward again. "What if I told you, you need not go any further?" His golden eyes motioned to the road behind her. "What if I told you, your journey could end here? That what you seek is not at the end of some treacherous road . . . but rather right in the palm of my hand??"

The woman couldn't look at him. He was lying. He had to be lying.

Pazari sighed dramatically, dragging a clawed hand down his face in exasperation.

"Ahh, but of course. Silly fox. Words mean so little to you, don't they, traveler? You're a woman of proof. Of action!"

His fluffy tail curled around his arm.

"Very well!"

His small hands moved to the side of his cart. A cabinet. She was certain it had not been there before. Then, his paws curled around the handle. With a soft creak, the doors swung open, and from within the darkened space, he reached inside.

Turning to her, and with a smile that shone like a thousand suns, he held up a small vial of an unknown liquid.

"Come. Come closer," Pazari purred. "And I will show you the closest thing to a miracle this world has ever known."

The vial glowed. A quiet, shimmering thing, turning softly between Pazari's claws. The woman could not look away. She was entranced by the liquid within.

The fluid was dark . . . midnight violet. But as the light hit it, it flickered, shifting like spilled oil in water. Like the shine from an abalone shell. It was wrong and unnatural, yet hypnotic.

Pazari observed her watching it, his smile static and plastered against his face.

"Fascinating, isn't it?" He turned the vial between his fingers once more, admiring its shimmer as well. "Such a small thing and yet, it holds a power greater than even the oldest magics. Better than any witch."

His golden eyes reflected a spark of giddiness as he said this.

The woman croaked, still enchanted by the mysterious vial. "Wh-what is it?"

Pazari let out a small hum. "This, dear traveler, is better than resurrection! Better than spells. Better than any ritual that a witch could ever dream to perform."

The woman's mouth felt even dryer.

Pazari lifted the vial higher, watching how the sunlight curled through it.

"It does not bring back the dead." His voice lowered, curling like vines. "It does something *far more* merciful."

He leaned forward once more.

"It erases them entirely."

The woman inhaled deeply at that revelation, and Pazari smiled at her response.

"Not just from memory though. But from the world itself," he continued.

His words slithered through the air,

snaking through her ears. She did not move as she processed.

He tilted his head, feigning sympathy.

"Oh poor traveler. I see it in you, you know." His voice was soft now, almost tender. "That grief. That weight. The way it drags at your steps. Sours every breath. Pulls at you like hands from the dark. I've seen that before, many, many times. Not good. Not good at all."

He tsked. "How long has it been since you've had a day without it? A moment where it has not lingered, gnawing at the edges of your mind?"

She said nothing still.

"You wake with it. You sleep with it. You choke on it." His claws tapped against the glass. "But you do not have to. Not with this."

The fox's voice dipped lower now. "Imagine, traveler. No more grief. No more loss. No more missing her, because she would have never existed."

His focus was fully locked on her, smiling, reading the hesitation in her green, sad eyes.

"You would not be 'forgetting' her, you know." He gestured loosely. "It would be as if she never was." A slow breath. His voice softened, curling into a lullaby-like cadence. "No gravestone. No small, empty bed. No aching space where her laughter once lived."

He sighed dramatically, tucking the vial close to his chest.

"Mmmm. Doesn't that sound . . ." His

golden eyes burned. "Peaceful?"

For a single, terrible moment, she thought yes.

Yes. It did sound peaceful. To wake up and never know this pain. To never have to live in its shadow. To be free. The thought was there, flickering like a dying match.

Pazari saw it. And he loved it.

"*Mmmm*. There it is."

Pazari sighed dreamily, shaking his head. The jewelry he wore clanked together as his head swayed.

"But of course, such relief is not without cost," he said, rolling the vial up and down the edge of his cart.

"Something this rare, this powerful, this fantastical . . . well. I can't just give it away, now can I?"

He looked down at the basket she had been holding close to her body.

"But I am always willing to trade."

The woman shook her head, snapping out of her daze. "I have nothing."

"Ohhh, but you do!"

"What?" She asked, annoyed.

"It is small. Barely worth mentioning . . ."

He pointed toward the small stuffed rabbit nestled between the quilt's folds.

"Something so loved," he mused. "Something so cherished."

He tapped the vial lightly against his long, white teeth. "Now, *that* is worth something, wouldn't you agree?"

"No. I do not. I should be going."

Pazari clicked his tongue. "Come now! Don't go! Surely you see the fairness of it?

A thing worn soft with love, exchanged for a world where pain does not exist? That item is old. Worn. Frayed at the edges." He leaned in. "But things well-loved are so much more valuable, don't you think?"

"Besides." His sharp teeth shined. "I do love rabbits."

The woman looked down at her bare feet on the dirt and let out a shaky breath. Maybe she should be done entertaining this fool of a fox?

Pazari studied her hesitation, her contemplation, eyes sharp as a blade.

He exhaled. "A shame."

His ears drooped, his tail curling against the wagon as he slowly turned from her back to his cart.

Then a thought. Suddenly, his pierced

ears perked up. "WAIT! Perhaps I have been unfair! After all, it is difficult to make such a decision without knowing its full effect, yes?"

Without waiting for her to answer, he tossed the vial in the air and snatched it with his other hand. Then, in a single, smooth movement . . . Pop! The cork came loose with a soft hiss. A thin wisp of violet smoke curled from the vial's mouth, twisting in the air like a beckoning finger. It shimmered as it rose, curling, whispering, reaching. Sparkling like popping fireworks encased in endless smoke.

Pazari's face lowered slyly as he lifted it beneath her nose, the fumes enveloping her face. The popping of sizzling carbonation smattered her nostrils.

"A small taste," he purred. "No charge."

Her body tensed as she tried to refuse. She tried holding her breath, but it was too late. The scent was too strong.

Warm. Familiar. Like nothing.

At first, it felt gentle. Like slipping into a warm bath. Like sinking into soft arms.

The weight of her being lifted like a cloud, and the knots in her mind loosened.

She exhaled, and the universe shifted all around her.

A memory.

Folding tiny little dresses in her hands.

Marveling at the smallest socks she'd ever seen.

A baby cooing in the corner bassinet.

She smiles and looks, but nothing is there.

She looks down.

The dresses in her hands are now gone, replaced with simple tea towels.

She had only been folding tea towels.

Another memory.

She stands in her small kitchen, bathed in orange morning light. The scent of lavender and sugar fills the space. Flour covers the kitchen counter. Tiny hands press into soft dough beside hers.

"Mommy, look!"

She turns, but the counter is empty.

No flour-streaked cheeks. No dimpled fingers stealing blueberry bits.

The rolling pin sits idle. The handprint in the flour vanished.

She blinks.

The warmth remains.

She bakes alone.

A new memory unlocked.

A field. A breeze. Wildflowers sway beneath a bright, blue sky.

A child is there. Running. Twirling. Arms stretching wide, gathering yellow petals in tiny hands.

But now . . .

The wind blows through nothing. The flowers do not stir.

But it had always been that way, hadn't it?

Then.

The swing.

It creaks softly, swaying in the breeze.

Once, a small girl had been there, legs kicking, grinning, calling out..

"Push me, Mommy!"

Now? Only an empty seat.

Nothing.

The memories shifted again.

A small picnic blanket spread beneath a crooked oak.

The two of them eating and drinking.

Two cups. Two plates.

Or was it one?

She was sitting alone.

Just her.

And it was nice.

Another memory.

The game of chase through the village streets…

Her hands reaching, grabbing at her daughter playfully…

But no daughter existed.

No laughter.

No warm weight in her arms.

No child.

The warmth in her chest wrapped a new memory.

The tea . . .

Butterfly pea blossoms and blueberry juice swirled in steaming water, turning it a deep, ocean blue.

Tiny hands had once cupped a warm mug, wide blue eyes marveling as they always had.

"Like magic!"

Except . . .

The second cup was gone.

She sat at the table alone.

She exhaled.

What a fine day.

Everything spun.

And then . . .

The water.

The river roaring.

Her heart pounding.

She was back.

That day.

The sky had been gray. The wind had howled.

She had not been paying attention.

A splash.

A scream.

Her head snaps up.

Her breath stops.

Small arms thrashing. Dark hair disappearing into the current.

No. No, no, no.

She runs.

She runs.

The cold hits her like a wall, teeth of ice closing over her skin, dragging her under.

She fights. Claws. Reaches.

Fingers brush. Slip. Grasp.

She surfaces with a limp body in her arms.

The river's pull fought her, trying to take her down again.

She held on.

She held on.

Then she was running.

Sprinting.

Wailing.

Her bare feet slap against the cobbled streets of the village. The soaked weight in her arms is heavy, unmoving.

"Help me!" she sobs. "Please, someone please help me!"

Villagers turn. Faces blur past her, stunned and frozen.

"Someone!" Her voice cracks with screams. "Anyone!"

She falls to her knees screaming.

Arms tear the child from her grip.

She reaches out.

But the girl does not move.

Her lips, blue.

Her hair, wet.

Her face . . .

Gone.

She wasn't there anymore.

A grave.

She stands before it, hands shaking.

But the name…

There was no name.

Only blank stone.

A hole in time.

Life was peaceful.

The warmth pressed deeper, smoothing the cracks.

A small, untouched bed.

A home wrapped in silence.

A woman, sitting at a table.

Drinking blue tea, alone.

She did not remember why.

She did not know who she had lost.

Only that something had been missing.

Something had always been missing.

But what?

It didn't matter.

Life was good.

The warmth whispered.

Nothing.

Nothing was missing.

It has always been this way. Just you.

Alone.

She exhaled and let go.

Just her.

Alone.

FLASH

Suddenly, the warmth was ripped away. A hand lifted from her face, and everything came crashing down. The air turned sharp.

Cold, biting and brutal.

Reality was a gut punch, and her mind gagged from the blow. She saw it all.

The river. The limp weight in her arms. The sprint through the streets. The grave.

Her daughter.

Her daughter.

Her daughter.

She collapsed to the ground in front of

the cart, as the basket hit the ground rolling. Her hands pressed into the dirt in front of her, as her lungs ceased function. The world swayed wildly. The edges of her vision darkened. Her chest caved inward and heaved. A noise clawed from her throat . . . a half-strangled gasp, a broken thing, desperate for air she could not reach.

But the air would not come. She could not breathe. She could not. Was she dying?

An exasperated sigh.

"Oh, dear traveler. That reaction was rather uncalled for I'd say. Very unbecoming."

A shadow shifted. A rustle of fabric. A whoosh of a fluffy tail.

She barely registered it. Her pulse thundered in her ears. Her vibrating fingers scratched into the ground.

Behind her, Pazari scoffed.

"Well. I see how it is," he muttered, brushing off his cloak. "Clearly, nothing I have is of interest to you."

The cabinet snapped shut. Glass clinked. Chains rattled. The soft creak of wood as he began packing up his wares, huffing in the process.

"Shame, really," he mused, half to himself. "I do so love a good trade."

His voice drifted, lazy, indifferent. He was over it.

But she barely heard him. Her hands trembled as she forced them to move. Slowly, she pressed her palms into the road and pushed herself up. Her body felt drained and heavy from what she had just experienced. She wiped at her face, dusting herself off.

She reached for her basket, clutching it as it was the only thing to bring her back to reality.

As she rose up, that's when she saw it. A glint. A flicker. From the corner of her eye, she saw. Amongst the cages. Amongst the rusted bars and rattling chains and shadowed things. She knew.

Pazari hummed behind her, lifting a crate onto his wagon as he packed up.

She straightened, turned, and finally spoke.

"Wait," she rasped. Still wobbly from the potion.

Pazari paused. Her shaky eyes meeting his unsympathetic gaze.

"I know what I want."

A slow smile molded across his face.

"I know what I want to trade. I know what I want to bargain for."

"Hm?" Pazari scrunched his nose at her.

"Him. There. That one." Her hand barely lifted as she pointed toward an unassuming cage. A small, black bird perched inside. Dark and ruffled. Pacing on thin, sharp talons. His beady, red eyes peering back at her.

A crow.

Pazari swiveled his head to the cage and back at her in confusion. "Oh, him?"

He nudged the cage with his elbow, just enough to make it rattle. The bird flapped violently, wings slamming against the bars. A sharp, furious hissing caw tore from its beak.

Pazari smirked at the reaction. He enjoyed it.

"Pfft. Poor little thing. Lost. Small. Angry." He clicked his tongue as his mischievous, narrow eyes flicked back to her, winking.

"Sound familiar?"

The woman fidgeted at his accusation.

Pazari chuckled at her silence. A knowing, wicked thing.

Then, with a lazy flourish, he reached behind him, rummaging through his collection of wares.

"You know," he said, his mocking tone wrapping around them, "he also came with the most delightful little mask!"

His hand emerged, and in it was red,

round, and beaked.

Ikari's mask. The one he had worn when she first met him.

Pazari twirled it between his fast moving fingers, rolling it idly from claw to claw. With a theatrical huff, he pressed it to his own face and grinned. Then, with a flick of his wrist, tossed it over his shoulder like garbage, as it clattered somewhere into the depths of his cart.

"I mean it," she demanded.

Pazari groaned at her words. "No. No, no, no. There's no way you want him."

He waved a dismissive hand at the cage.

"This crow? This menace? This absolute pain in my tail? Oh, traveler, I assure you, he is not worth it."

He suspired again, grander this time,

rolling his shoulders as if exhausted from this entire interaction.

"I have suffered years of his nonsense. His tricks, his sharp little beak, his constant, furious cawing. Begging for food like an endless pit. He's honestly just plain rude."

He shuddered.

"And now—he's mine." His foxy grin returned, sharper now. "And I quite like having him exactly where he is."

The woman lifted her chin, looking straight at the merchant before her.

"I want him, Pazari."

The fox blinked. Paused. Stared. Then barked out a laugh. A bright, surprised sound.

"You really want him free?" He gestured

wildly at the cage. "Seriously? Oh, dear traveler, you wound me! Have I not offered you far better things? Things of vast power? Far more significant than an angry little crow? Come now. Do not be daft. Do not ruse me!"

She said nothing.

Pazari squinted and leaned forward. Examined her face, as if searching for some kind of trick.

But there was no trick, only certainty. His lips pursed.

"Well . . . hmm," he muttered, scratching his head. "Alright then. I won't judge."

He paused a moment as if deep in thought,

"But. A trade, is a trade. A bargain, a

bargain."

The woman stalled, her hand petting the object of Pazari's desire. Slowly, her hand reluctantly curled around the item. Her fingers brushed against soft, well-worn fur.

The stuffed rabbit. The last remnant of her daughter's embrace.

She lifted it to her face and breathed in deeply. Faint. Lingering.

Her scent.

The scent of many days of play. Of days of love, and nights of cuddles. Then, with closed eyes, she extended it.

Pazari's paw quickly closed around it, snatching it from her, stealing her moment.

"Oh," he cooed, cradling the rabbit against his cheek. "Have I mentioned how much I love rabbits?"

And with a snap of his fingers, the cage door creaked open and the prisoner exploded out. A streak of black against the sky, wings slicing upward, vanishing into the trees above.

The woman inhaled, watching him go. A shadow against the clouds, and he was gone.

But before she could verbalize her thoughts, Pazari spoke again.

"The place you seek is on the left path. But, I must say . . . it is best you find somewhere warm, traveler. The storm is coming."

His voice deepened, serious and gentle in a way he had not been since the moment they had met. He continued, "And she is not kind."

The woman lifted an eyebrow, puzzled.

"Storm? Its seems fine out h—" The wind cut off her words. Cold. Sharp.

She blinked, and he was gone.

Cart. Trinkets. Cages. Pazari.

All gone. Like he had never been there at all.

Only the empty road remained. And the sky. Darkening. Bruising. The wind howled. And she knew.

A storm was coming.

THE BEAR

It began with her breath. A soft, silvery cloud curling into the night air, fading as soon as it formed. As she walked up the path, now curling towards a mountain, she looked at the trees around her. Once dark and towering, now growing skeletal. Ice rimmed their branches, their bark graying like slate.

She wrapped the quilted blanket around herself over her cloak, but it was useless. The warmth had long since been stolen from the fabric, leaving nothing but a thin barrier between her and the cold.

She shivered. She had thought she knew what freezing was. The wind that had brushed against her bare skin at night, the lonely chill of an empty home. But this? This was so very different. This was the kind of cold that seeped through skin and into the soul. The kind of cold that did not leave.

She tried to move faster, to keep the blood in her limbs from slowing, but her unclad feet felt heavier with each step. Her hands had long since gone numb, the muscles stiff, barely obeying her commands.

A single, delicate snowflake drifted through the empty sky, landing soundlessly upon her sleeve.

And another.

Then more.

She watched as the world went pale, as the frost along the trees thickened, as her cloak stiffened with the gathering ice. A dull ache throbbed in her limbs, sluggish and deep. Her eyelashes grew heavy.

She blinked, and tiny shards of frost fell from her lashes.

She could not feel her toes. Or her nose. Or her lips.

It was too cold. Too still. Too quiet.

The ice around her crept settled into the cracks of the earth like veins of glass. Her bare feet crunched against the hardening dirt, each step more brittle than the last.

As if meaning to disrupt her thoughts, a raindrop appeared.

The snowflakes had changed. Heavier now.

Small. Salted.

One struck her cheek, warm against the cold, slipping down her skin, like a tear not her own.

Another followed. Then another.

Not enough to break the ice gripping the land, but enough to warn her—things were about to get worse.

She dropped her basket. She no longer needed it. All she had was the blanket. The quilt was her cocoon.

She pressed forward. Each step a battle

against the creeping frost.

And then, through the haze of white and gray, she saw it.

As if created just for her.

A cave.

A circle of black in the distance, carved into the mountainside. Beckoning. Waiting. Watching.

The forest had grown barren. Nothing but dead trees and ice-coated ground stretched before her.

There was no shelter, no warmth.

Her body screamed for relief from the pain of the ice. From the oncoming water.

From the storm.

And so, with a final, reluctant breath, she moved her frigid being toward the shelter and stepped inside.

As she walked within it, the first thing she noticed was the smell. An overbearing odor of old fur, damp earth, and something stale . . . something forgotten . . . something familiar.

She took a slow step forward. The deeper she moved into the cave, the more the dark settled around her. As if meant to jolt her senses, she heard a sound.

A long, slow exhale, like the mountains themselves were breathing. A massive figure stirred in the shadows. Giant and towering.

The large shape of something curled in on itself, shifting beneath thick, heavy fur. It smelled like damp moss, and pungent earth.

Then, two eyes opened. Not normal eyes, glowing eyes. A pale, weary blue, burning faintly in the dark.

The huge creature yawned.

A bear. It was a bear. Well, something shaped like one.

It was probably five times the size of any bear the woman had seen before or at least read about. Almost as large as some of the trees she had walked through just moments prior. He was surrounded by heaps and heaps of cloth, furs, pillows, and blankets, and wore what looked like a light blue nightgown. The white creature was a mix of something terrifying, odd, and . . . relaxing.

It stretched, massive paws flexing as it slowly and lazily sat up, blinking at her.

With a voice as deep and slow as rolling thunder, he finally spoke, "What a mistake you've made."

The woman tensed, stopping any further movement in the cave.

The bear let out a slow sigh, adjusting the threadbare pillow beneath one arm, his massive claws dragging across the cave floor.

"It's far too cold out there," he grumbled, eyes already half-lidding again. "Far too miserable. Why suffer?"

His head lolled to the side.

"Better to stay inside."

The woman gulped at her predicament, hoping he wasn't a hungry bear.

"I only seek shelter for a moment."

The bear huffed, shifting beneath his long, sagging white fur. The dim glow of his bright, blue eyes flickered for a bit.

"A moment?" he echoed. "Eh . . . Hmph. That's what they all say."

She frowned. "They?"

"The ones who come here," he rumbled under his breath. "The ones who enter. They always say they will leave soon." His massive paw stretched, pressing into the cold ground beside him as he yawned.

"And yet . . ." his voice dragged, his wide head flopping to the side half-awake, "they never do."

The woman took a slow step back as the bear blinked at her, lazy and unimpressed.

"Look at you, small human," he said, motioning vaguely with his large paw. "Cold and tired. You'll never make it out there."

He let out another slow, defeated, heavy-winded sigh.

"Better to just sleep. Better to stay."

The woman bit her cheek. "I can't."

"Why not?" the bear asked, repositioning, settling deeper into his mound of furs and cloth that surrounded him.

"I have somewhere I need to be."

"Why?"

She hesitated. The bear stared at her. Waiting for an answer. A deep quiet filled the space between them.

Then, softly, lazily he asked, "What's the point?" The bear exhaled, his voice low and slow and achingly tired. "Outside is cold. Wet. Miserable." His glowing blue eyes radiated brightly in the dark as they looked down upon the woman. "There is nothing good out there. No warmth. No comfort. Just stay with me. Stay with Khwam."

He looked at the wall of his cave and huffed.

"Why leave here? It is comfortable."

Silence.

The woman looked at Khwam, then

back at her surroundings. She hadn't really noticed it until her eyes had fully adjusted to the dark. But then, she saw them.

The "others" Khwam had spoken of.

Shapes barely visible in the dim light, scattered across the cave floor.

Bones.

Curled figures, slumped in corners. Some still draped in rotted cloth. A shoe. A skeletal hand resting near a blanket, stiff and unmoving.

The woman gagged.

They had not been killed. They had simply never left. They had curled up beside the bear, closed their eyes and never opened them again.

Khwam let out a slow, long breath, watching her reaction with an emotionless curiosity.

"You understand now, human," he stated. "It is peaceful here."

Her body was now shaking. Not from the cold, but from what this cave felt like. How familiar it seemed.

Her eyes swept across the space. A sink, or what might have once been one, was piled high with filthy dishes, crusted with the remnants of long-forgotten meals. The furniture lay in pieces, shattered and splintered, some half-buried beneath old, tattered blankets.

The smell was worse though. A deep, cloying stench of mildew, thick and suffocating, like river-soaked clothes left to rot. It had become more and more unbearable as she remained in that space. It clung to the damp air, to the cave walls, to the thick fur of the creature that lay before her.

A strange, sinking exhaustion pulled at her limbs as she surveyed the cave.

Her legs ached. Her body longed for rest.

The cave was warm. She could just sit. Just close her eyes. Just for a moment.

She rubbed the quilt between her fingertips, feeling its softness. Perhaps she could use this to take just a small nap? Maybe Khwam was right?

Her body ached in a way that had nothing to do with the cold outside. She could feel it now. The pain wasn't sharp, it wasn't screaming. It was dull, constant, something she had carried for so long that she no longer noticed the weight of it. But now, here, where the wind did not reach, where the frost could not creep in, she could feel it. All of it.

She lowered herself to the stone floor. Just for a moment. Just to rest.

The quilt, still wrapped around her, smelled of home. Of all the things she had lost. It still held warmth, though she knew it was not from her. She rubbed the fabric between her fingers, feeling the softness of it again, tracing the stitching. Taking it in.

Her eyes blurred as she followed the threads.

So many colors. So many pieces. Each

one a fragment, a memory stitched together with love.

She remembered.

A castle made from chairs and pillows. A small voice calling, "Mommy, you can't come in unless you say the password!"

A tent beneath the stars, whispering fantastical stories under the blanket's cover. A sick day, curled on the couch, warm, blue tea in her hands. Small fingers tugging at the quilt, as a little girl burrowed beneath it with her.

She could bury herself in these memories. In the quilt. Wrap herself up, hide within it. Cocoon herself away from everything and everyone.

"Sleep," Khwam said as he looked down at her curled figure on the ground.

"When you sleep, there is no more pain."

She had walked so far. Did it even matter anymore? Did the Witch even matter anymore? Nothing mattered.

If she closed her eyes now, perhaps she wouldn't have to open them again.

The storm outside raged on, the wind howling through the  mouth of the cave. But in here, it was quiet. Safe.

Perhaps Khwam was right.

Perhaps there was no reason to fight anymore.

She curled into herself more, pressing her face into the quilt, letting the darkness around her sink into her bones.

She closed her eyes.

Just for a moment.

The cold whispered.

"Lie down."

It wouldn't be so bad.

Just a moment to rest. Just a moment to stop moving.

"Lie down."

No one would find her here.

No one would whisper her name.

No one would say, "Poor thing, she never moved on."

No one would pity her.

Just for a moment.

She would sleep.

NO.

Her eyes snapped open.

NO!

She shot upright, gasping, clawing at the quilt as if it had tried to strangle her. She almost let it take her.

Khwam stared down at her, his blue eyes peering into her.

Her mind had wandered too far. Had drifted too close to something she could not return from.

The warmth was a lie.

The comfort was a trap.

She was not safe here.

She could not stay here.

She would not be like them, she thought, as she looked at the bones scattered around her.

NO.

She faced the great, lumbering creature, slouched beneath his own weight. His body draped across a mound of soft things, a nest of comfort.

This creature was not happy. He was trapped. He was sad.

Caged.

His great, sluggish breath filled the cavern. His sorrow so vast, it had become a physical thing.

Slow and heavy. A lullaby of despair.

The woman stood up and stepped forward. Her hands still holding her daughters quilt.

The last item.

"What are you doing, human? Why do

you not sleep, and ignore it all? Ignore the world?" Khwam quietly asked.

Her hand gripped the blanket draped over her shoulders, looking up at the mass that was Khwam.

Then, softly, she spoke up, "Because there is sunlight."

The bear let out a slow, rumbling humph.

"But it is cold outside," he countered.

"And yet, the sun will return," she retorted

He let out a long, drawn-out sigh, shifting his pillow again. Fluffing it. Irritated at her responses.

"Outside is empty."

"But it is open."

"Outside is lonely."

She hesitated. "But it is free."

He stared at her, then spoke again. "Life is painful."

"But it matters." She exhaled.

A slow blink.

"Pain is heavy."

"So is love."

Another long silence.

His great chest rose, then fell.

"The weight never leaves. Memories hurt."

"But they are worth remembering."

"Well, memories fade and disappear."

"Then . . . I will make new ones."

Khwam's nose twitched at her answer. For the first time, he did not respond immediately. His tired, glowing blue eyes rested on her, unreadable.

His gaze followed her movements, blinking in slow surprise, not speaking a word again. Then, with careful hands, she lifted the quilted blanket from her shoulders. She stepped closer, placing it gently over the bear's hunched, slouched form.

His gigantic body stilled, and his great breath paused for just a moment. A slow puff of air exited from his mouth. He sighed loudly, burying himself beneath the fabric, his great, wide paws sinking deeper into its warmth, snuggling in like a baby.

And the glowing in his eyes dimmed as he laid his weepy head down. Being so close to him now, she could see it. His face was soaked.

He had been silently crying this entire

time.

With a final sigh, he spoke one last time.

"You are stronger than I was."

And with that, he slept.

THE STORM

The woman turned her face to the opening of the cave. She was empty now. She had nothing left to carry. But, she had to continue onward. She had made it this far. The Witch would help her.

She knew it. She had to.

With a solid determination, she walked out of the cave, and into the frigid air.

Dark clouds had claimed the sky and churned in the distance above her.

Smack.

The first raindrop had been fairly small. Barely there.

But the taste? Salty.

It clung to her lips like the tears she had refused to shed. Like the ones she had swallowed down, night after night, alone in that house of dust and ghosts.

Another drop. Then another. Each one a sharp, stinging needle against her raw skin. She had no protection now. No quilt. No basket. No items.

Just her.

Then, as if on cue, the heavens split apart, and the sky wept. Screaming down on her in a flood of water. Slamming against the earth, pushing against her like unseen hands, demanding she kneel before it.

And the woman screamed back.

Her voice ripped through the air, hoarse and broken, swallowed whole by the roar of the storm. It wailed loudly, howling through the trees around her, shrieking in the wind. The rain lashed at her, beating her down, soaking through the remaining layers she had wrapped so tightly around herself.

She was drenched. Water dripped from her hair, droplets covering her vision. Water seeping into her mouth. She spit them out, gasping as she pushed forward. The icy cold sliced into her blood, deeper than anything she had ever felt before. Deeper than the ice she had walked through just hours ago.

No. That wasn't true. She had felt something colder.

Her daughter's body in her arms.

Limp. Dripping. Tiny, ice cold fingers, lips tinted blue, hair tangled and slick against her once rosy cheeks. The weight of her, heavier than she had ever been in life. Her small chest did not rise. Did not fall. Did not stir with breath or warmth of existence. Just cold and gone.

Unforgiving. Permanent. Final.

She had screamed then, too.

Just like this.

Her foot slipped. Mud swallowing her bare skin, pulling her down. She hit the ground, hard, elbows slamming against slick stone. Pain shot through her arms, but she did not stop. She could not stop. Hands weak, she pushed herself up, her soaked cloak dragging behind her like a funeral veil. Waterlogged, heavy as a ball and chain.

Another step. Then another.

The wind raged around her.

The mountain climbed higher, steeper. The path blurred, swallowed by the downpour, by the thick, heavy mist enveloping her naked feet. The world vanished in sheets of silver and flashes of lighting.

Her body shouted for her to stop. To return to the cave.

She refused.

The storm bore down, whispering its taunts, its doubts. It tried to break her. To drown her, just as the river had her child. Just as the world had the moment she had lost the only thing that had ever mattered.

She kept climbing, looking up occasionally and belting back at nature's wrath. Through the curtain of rain, she saw it. A shape in the storm.

A face.

A woman's face, lamenting, her mouth open in an eternal cry, her eyes sunken and endless. The clouds swirled around her, her sorrow twisting into the wind, clinging to the heavens. A face not too dissimilar from her own. Or maybe it was her own.

She could not tell.

The wind did not howl. It sobbed.

A thousand voices. A thousand cries, layered upon each other. Screaming. Bawling. A chorus of pain, of agony that had existed long before her and would exist long after. The voices of all who had made this journey, of all who had stood where she stood, of all who had lost and would lose again. Of ones who would make that journey still.

And among them, her own.

A wretched, broken thing, carried off into the wind, lost among the countless others who had screamed before her.

She would suffer this water. Just as her daughter had suffered by the hands of the same merciless force of nature.

The world was drowning.

Or perhaps, she was drowning.

This rain would not let up. It struck the earth in torrents, rushing down the steep incline like a river, carving a path of mud and stone beneath her, ensuring she would slip.

She stumbled forward. Again, and again. Every move forward was agony.

Her body collapsed, drained. The storm

had stripped her bare, beaten her raw, but still . . . still, she pressed on. She had to.

Lightning split the sky. For the briefest moment, the world was illuminated in a stark, brilliant flash of white. And as it brightened the land around her, she saw it.

A shape in the distance. A cottage.

It was small, unassuming, nestled in the mountainside, half-lost in the torrential mist of rain. Dots of golden light seeped through her eyes. Windows. Warmth.

A promise.

She gasped, the sight of it striking her harder than the storm itself.

She was close. She was so close. Was she close?

Her feet moved of their own accord now, dragging her forward. The incline steepened, the ground turning even more treacherous beneath her bare feet, slick with mud and rain. She clawed her way up, fingers slipping against the wet rocks.

She was so close.

Her fingernails cracked, split, tore against the unyielding rocks she clambered up, but she did not stop. She couldn't. Even as pain lanced through her fingertips, even as the sharp sting of broken nails bled into the storm, she kept climbing.

She was so close.

The wind roared in her ears, but the cottage was there, just ahead. Just a few more steps.

She was so close.

Another gust slammed into her. She rolled down the hill, her body smacking into rocks and trees. Covering her in mud. But this wouldn't stop her.

She was so close.

After what felt like hours, she staggered, nearly falling, but she caught herself against a crooked wooden post. The remains of a broken fence. Her fingers clutched at it, her vision hazy.

She was so close.

The cottage door was only a few feet away.

She reached for it.

Her hand barely grazed the handle before the remaining strength she had finally failed her.

Her knees buckled, and her body crumpled forward, spilling onto the front steps.

The world swayed. The warmth was so close now.

Through the focus of her fading vision, she saw the door creak open.

Light spilled onto the porch.

A figure stood within it, shadowed above her.

A soft breath of warmth gently kissed her frozen skin. She looked up, right as it all finally enveloped her.

Darkness.

# THE WITCH

She awoke to warmth.

For the first time in what felt like years,
she was cozy. No biting cold seeping
through her skin, no ice burrowing into her
bones. Only the gentle welcome of heat, of
stillness, of something so achingly soft she
almost wept at the sensation: the
embracing weight of a thick quilt

enveloped her, the caring hush of a quiet home.

A lantern flickered beside her, casting golden pools of light along the walls, its glow swaying with the quiet rhythm of the room.

Something simmered in the hearth nearby, its faint aroma curling through the air. Herbs, something floral, and something faintly familiar. Something peaceful.

It was a comfort. A true, undeniable comfort. Finally.

Rubbing her eyes, she took in the cottage. It was small, and quiet. An oasis nestled in the heart of the mountain.

Flower pots and books adorned the room. The sofa she had been resting on was soft, adorned with wool blankets and cotton throws. The air smelled of incense and aged wood, yet another, perfect smell graced her senses.

Blueberry butterfly pea tea.

She turned her head, and there, beside the fire, sat a woman.

The Witch.

She was older, perhaps, but not frail. Not weak in the slightest, but powerful. An essence of strength radiated from her. She was content.

As the woman looked around, she did not see them. The bottles of potions. Items of magic. Books of spells. Nothing.

Just a nice, quiet home.

The Witch before her had red hair and kind blue eyes. Her fair, freckled hands moved silently, pouring two cups of the deep indigo liquid. Spritzing the tea with a slice of lemon, the color changed to a dramatic purple. The steam curled into the air, vanishing before it could reach the ceiling.

"Drink," the Witch offered.

The woman did not move at first. She

only sat there, staring, unsure whether to speak or simply exist in this fragile, unique moment.

Then, hesitantly, she reached forward, taking the offered cup into cold-stung fingers. It was warm against her mud-caked skin. Was this a potion, disguised as tea?

The cup was smooth against her skin, grounding. Real. She lifted it to her lips, and the first sip unlocked something deep within her chest.

It was. It was just tea. And it was amazing.

The woman had made it.

"You have traveled far," the Witch spoke knowingly.

The woman clutched the cup closer to

her body as she looked at the woman in front of her.

"I want her back."

Silence.

"Do you?"

The woman blinked.

Of course I . . .”

Her words faltered.

The Witch waited.

Looking down, she was suddenly hit with her journeys failure.

Her items. Gone. Taken. Given away. Abandoned.

She did not realize she was crying until she tasted the salt of her own tears mingling with the tea in her hand.

“I have nothing,” she croaked, her voice breaking. “I have nothing left to offer.”

The woman could not look the Witch in the eyes. She was sure she was being judged and would be cast out. Unworthy of the shelter she had stumbled into.

The Witch across from her only smiled. "Then you have brought everything."

The woman choked out a soft, broken laugh, shaking her head. "No. I have failed! Oh, Witch! The items! I . . . I . ."

"Were never the key," the Witch interrupted gently. "The essence of your loss was never in them." She placed a careful finger against the woman's chest. "It has always been here."

The woman looked down at her torn clothing, as if she might shatter beneath the weight of those words. For so long, she had thought—had convinced herself—that, if she could only bring the right pieces, she could fix what had been broken. But nothing had ever been broken to begin with, except her.

Only lost.

And some losses cannot be undone.

She shuddered as the warmth awakened her more, pressing the cup against her lips again. The heat of the tea, of the fire, of the truth sinking into her body.

For a long time, they both said nothing. They just sipped tea.

Then, softly, hesitantly, the woman spoke. "In the forest and on the path, I met a crow. And a fox. And a bear . . . and—"

The Witch chuckled, shaking her head as she interrupted. "Oh, Ikari, Pazari, and Khwam. Dear old friends of mine."

The woman looked at her, bewildered. *"Friends?* You know them?"

"Oh yes. They linger, don't they?" the woman mused. "Even now, I'm sure you can still feel them." She stirred her tea absently with a spoon. "They never truly leave, you know. Even here, even now, you'll hear Ikari's caws in the distance. You'll feel Pazari's sly little gaze when you least expect it. You'll wake some mornings, convinced Khwam is next to you, whispering in your ear."

She glanced up, meeting the woman's puffy eyes. "They do not vanish, dear. But here? Here, you just learn how to live with them."

The woman swallowed the last bits of her tea. It reminded her of her daughter.

And it was a comfort.

As she set the tea cup down on the table in front of her, she looked at the Witch again. She seemed so . . . normal.

As if knowing her thoughts, the Witch spoke to her, her eyes shining in the fireplace light. "I am no Witch, dear."

The woman looked down and pursed

her lips.

"When I first stood here. When I found myself in this place," the Witch began, "I was just as you are now."

The woman looked up.

"My hands were empty. My heart, heavier than the mountain itself." The Witch exhaled, staring into the fire as if she could see something beyond it. "I believed this place could offer me what I had lost."

She gestured around the cozy, candlelit room, the flicker of firelight dancing in her eyes.

"I, too, once searched for a way to undo the past. I came here thinking there would be magic strong enough to bring back the one I loved. That if I could just walk far enough, suffer long enough, prove myself worthy enough—somewhere, someone would make me whole again."

The Witch smiled longingly.

"But in the end," the Witch continued, "it was not magic that changed me. It was understanding that their love did not die with them."

She wiped away a tear. "It lived on, woven into my being."

The fireplace danced softly, glowing golden flickers against the Witch's face.

"I walked the path just as you did. I met them, just as you did. Those interesting creatures." The Witch's eyes met hers.

She tilted her head slightly, as if she could see the image forming behind the woman's eyes. "The forest was never a place of guidance," she murmured. "It was a place of longing. It takes what the heart cannot release and breathes it back into the world, a whisper of what once was."

The woman shivered. "I saw her."

"You saw what you wanted to see."

The words cut deeper than she had expected.

The Witch did not soften them. "Denial is the gentlest of all grief's faces," she said. "It does not rage, nor weep, nor plead. It only lingers. It lets you believe, just for a little while, that nothing has changed. That if you just step forward, she will be there. But the moment you reach for her, she slips away."

The Witch let the words sink in. "That was never her, sweetheart, That was your grief, wrapped in the shape of her face."

The woman clenched her hands into fists, silently.

The Witch placed her hand on the woman's. "The forest showed you what you were not ready to lose. But ghosts do not carry the living forward. Only the living can do that, dear."

The woman nodded.

"Ikari's hunger," the Witch continued, "was never for your daughter. It was for your own self-hatred."

The woman bit her lip.

"You have carried your guilt like an albatross, feeding it, letting it consume you." The Witch's voice was gentle, but firm.

"Ikari was the part of you that starved for atonement. That lashed out in rage because the weight of your guilt was too much to bear."

The woman looked down at her hands as she fidgeted with the cushion, remembering the way Ikari had snarled at her. Accusing her, blaming her.

"YOU LET HER GO!" He had screamed.

"You did not kill your daughter," the Witch said. "But you have been punishing yourself as if you *had*."

Tears welled in the woman's eyes.

The Witch did not stop.

"And Pazari's bargain was never about forgetting her . . . but forgetting yourself."

The woman sniffled.

"He knew your weakness," the Witch continued. "That part of you that believed if you erased the pain, you could erase the loss. That the weight of grief was too much to bear, so why not simply bargain it away?"

The fragrance from the vial returned to her nose, stinging it for just a moment as she recalled that interaction. Sniffling again.

"But loss is not meant to be erased or bargained for," the Witch said. "It is meant to be carried."

The woman nodded, almost imperceptibly.

"And then there was Khwam."

The Bear.

The endless cold. The weight of exhaustion so deep she almost did not rise.

"Khwam did not try to harm you. Did not try to steal from you. Khwam only asked for one thing."

The woman's lips trembled.

"He asked for you to just…stop. You see, despair is a stillness," the Witch said. "A place where grief becomes so vast that moving forward seems impossible."

She looked toward the door, as if staring at something beyond it. "There was a moment when you almost did not leave that cave, wasn't there?"

The woman nodded.

"You thought, perhaps, it would be easier to stop walking altogether."

The woman recalled how tired she had felt. How badly she just wanted to sleep.

"Lie down,' Khwam had coaxed. But you didn't." The Witch turned to her again. "Because even then, you still carried her with you. And you knew that if you did, her memory might fade. That isn't something you would *ever* allow to happen. Her existence was too important."

A tear slipped down the woman's cheek.

"You did not fail by trading those items," the Witch said. "You succeeded by carrying her in your heart, even when the world tried to make you forget."

The woman had traveled so far.

Suffered so much.

And all this time, she had thought she was trying to bring her daughter back.

But she wasn't.

She was trying to bring herself back.

The Witch's voice relaxed.

"This was never about finding her again.

It was about learning to live without her."

The Witch let out a long sigh, staring at the hearth, if looking beyond the walls of the cottage, beyond the years that had passed.

"After my journey, when I first arrived as this wonderful, wonderful place, I found only a man. An old traveler, much like me and much like you. He did not offer me magic, nor miracles. Only a place to rest, for as long as I needed, until I was ready to leave."

She turned back to the woman, bowing her head. "I offer you that same kindness, for I think I am now ready to depart."

The woman could not believe her ears. "You're . . . leaving?"

The Witch nodded. "The path calls me

home. I no longer need the safe dwelling of this cottage. For I believe I can bring that comfort with me now. I can now finally return home. Back to the village,"

The woman interjected. "But I just arrived? And the villagers . . . they feared you. They said—"

"Oh dear, they do not understand," the Witch interrupted. "The villagers? They are the ones who blindly tuck away from reality. They are the ones who have just not made this journey yet." She reached for her cloak hung near the door, draping it over her shoulders. "And until they do, they will never understand."

The woman looked down at her tea, at the faint reflections swimming in the deep blue. "And what about me?" she asked quietly. "What happens now?"

The woman smiled. "This home is yours for as long as you need it, dear. You will have everything you could ever need here," she said. "Until the path calls you back home, like it has to me."

The fire crackled, filling the silent space between them. "You will know when it's time. And our friends may stop by from time to time. Hell, it may even rain occasionally. The storms can be brutal. But you can remain here as long as your heart desires, sweetheart. You will always be safe here."

The woman swallowed. "And if another comes?"

The Witch gave a knowing look. "They *will* come, just as you have," she said.

"And when they do, you will be there, tea in hand and a place for them to rest."

This place was small, humble, and simple. And yet, for the first time since her daughter's death, she felt no need to run.

The Witch rose, stepping toward the door. Her dark purple cloak was already wrapped around her, her small bag of belongings tucked beneath her arm. The woman followed her, hesitantly, as if she might change her mind and stay after all. To keep her company.

The door creaked open.

Cold air rushed inside, but it no longer bit as sharply as before. It was now sunny. Green. Beautiful.

The storm had passed. The path, though still slick with rain, stretched onward, waiting for her.

The Witch lingered in the doorway, breathing in the morning air. She turned once more, looking over the cottage with a quiet fondness.

Then, as if deciding something, she spoke again.

"The fire never goes out," she said softly, her kind eyes moving toward the flames inside. "You'll always be warm here."

She turned back to the woman, a knowing twinkle dancing within her eyes.

"One day, the path home will call your name, just as it did mine."

The woman looked at her and smiled. A true, genuine smile. For once, in a long time, she was happy. Content.

The Witch stepped forward, through the

doorway, onto the dew-covered path, and departed the cottage she had called home for so long.

As she walked down the trail, she did not look back. The mountain swallowed her silhouette, the rising fog curling around her until she was gone.

The woman stood in the doorway for a long time, watching until there was nothing left to see. Then she shut the door.

She exhaled, long and slow, pressing a hand against the worn wooden table in front of her to steady herself. Her posture straightened. Her shoulders relaxed. An undeniable weightlessness.

She had been carrying ghosts.

And now, she carried nothing.

Her eyes slid to a wall adorned with

paintings and flowers, and amongst them, a large mirror.

It hadn't been there before, she realized. Or, perhaps it had always been there. Tucked into the shadows, overlooked, forgotten. Its glass was clouded with dust, the frame worn and splintering at the edges.

She wasn't sure why she moved toward it. Maybe it was a need, a desire. The pull of seeing oneself after a long journey. Or maybe it was something deeper.

She stepped closer and looked.

The reflection was hazy at first, a shifting blur of shapes. She reached out with her dirty hand, swiping across the surface as the dust fell away.

And she saw herself.

Not as she had expected. The woman in the mirror was not the same one who had left the village.

Her once emerald cloak was tattered now, its fabric stained from mud. Her long hair had lost its softness, tangled with the wind, with the journey, with the things she had let go.

But it was her eyes that froze her in place.

They were not tired.

Not grieving.

Not longing.

They were quiet. Deep. Knowing.

Accepting.

For a fleeting, breathless moment, she thought it was—the Witch.

The Witch had come back.

The Witch had returned.

Her lips parted, a question forming . . . some instinct to call out, to name the figure before her and speak.

But this reflection moved when she did.

The same breath. The same hesitation.

There was no one else in the room..

It was just her.

In this cottage of embracing warmth,

was the woman, as she was.

And that, was enough.

AFTERWARD

To me, grief isn't a single emotion. It's a damn labyrinth. A constantly shifting.. *thing.*
Unpredictable and consuming. It lingers in the quiet moments. In the spaces left behind, and in the memories we can't bear to part with.
And I hate it… most times.

I wrote Evermourne after a series of moments seemed to collide all at once. A few weeks before I began, I had been watching a few Studio Ghibli animated films and clips, and something about their worlds sparked something. Their quiet magic, their sense of melancholy and wonder just stuck with me.

Then, I came across a true story that I couldn't shake out of my head at all..

A young woman in Japan had refused to throw away a pot of stew that had been sitting in her freezer for five years. It was the last meal her mother had made before suddenly passing away, and she couldn't bear to part with it. For years, her father told her to throw it out, but she wouldn't. Then, a television show brought in a renowned chef, who did something incredible.

He brought the stew **back to life.**

Like, he made it edible again, just as her mother had prepared it. And as she and her father sat together and ate, they wept. The weight of those years, of holding onto something so tangible, finally broke.

It was such a cathartic moment, and so beautiful to witness. This stew, that represented this woman's grief that she held onto, finally released in an absolutely astounding way.

It made me ponder my own grief, and the

way I hadn't really faced it head on. I thought about all the people I had lost within the past few years. Tugging within the back of my mind.

And I thought, as I watched the host, chef, woman and her father cry on my computer screen…what if this were a story? A mystical, Studio Ghibli-like journey, where a woman sets off to find someone who could bring something back to life? At first, it was a stew (real creative I know). Then, it became a basket of cherished items instead. The chef became a witch. And instead of a woman grieving her mother, what if she had lost her child?

But I needed obstacles for this woman. An encounter with a no-face type entity. Something that represented me in a way.

Well, I love crows. And I do have a bit of a temper…

Suddenly, Ikari was born.

The angry crow. A trickster, a spirit, something desperate and consuming. And I realized..wasn't anger one of the five stages of grief? Like, what if every obstacle she faced was a physical embodiment of those stages?

THAT was the moment Evermourne was truly born.

Writing this story felt like discovering something ancient, like uncovering a fable that had always existed, waiting for someone to bring it back to life. It came to me naturally, effortlessly, like a whispered tale passed down through generations. Like a story that had been told long before, but somehow forgotten. Evermourne didn't feel new. It felt old. Like a fairytale lost to time, waiting to be remembered.

And maybe that's why, from the moment I started writing, I could see it. Every frame, every color, every movement. I didn't just write Evermourne, I watched it unfold in my mind, like a film waiting to exist.

One day, I hope to see this story fully realized as an animated short of some kind. A film that captures the haunting beauty, the weight of sorrow, and the flickering hope of its journey. The quiet, eerie stillness of the forest. The warm glow of the lantern-lit village. The terrifying shadows of Ikari as his monstrous form stretches beyond the firelight. Pazari and his theatrical essence. A crying Khwam in a dark cave. A battering storm. And a cozy realization of acceptance in a warm cottage.

The beautifully cyclical nature of grief incarnate.

I don't know when or how, but I know that someday, Evermourne will move.

Until then, it lives here. On these pages.

If you have ever carried the weight of grief, I hope this story resonated with you. And if you have not, I hope it serves as a glimpse into the shadows of the human heart. A place we will all find ourselves one day, whether we want to or not.

Thank you so much for reading.

~ *Wesley Eagle*

BONUS CONTENT

# CONCEPT ART

☙ IKARI ❧

Ikari started as a creepy dude in a crow mask, lurking like some kind of little plague doctor with bad intentions. Then I realized, why stop at a cool mask? Why not make him a full-on crow spirit? Crows are awesome.

And so, he became pure, undiluted Anger with feathers. His transformations reflect exactly how anger works: at first, he's just a snarky little bird-man, then he mutates into a looming nightmare, and finally, he goes full apocalyptic fire-demon mode.

Sometimes, anger doesn't stop until it burns everything down.

I even considered giving him a staff or walking stick at one point, but he'd probably just use it to beat people he didn't like.

Have a
staff?
Isari:
The
Crow Spirit
Huge now
Venom-like

PAZARI

Pazari was tricky at first because I couldn't decide if he should be menacing and creepy, or adorable and weirdly charming.

So I picked both. He's a flamboyant, over-the-top fox dripping in gold necklaces and earrings. He's got that fast-talking, deal-making, "trust me, pal" energy, like magical used-car salesman who know he's scamming you, but still expects you to be impressed.

This fella represents Bargaining, and not just for the protagonist. He'll haggle with literally anyone if it means making a deal…and if they're on his path.

At one point, I debated whether he should have The Woman's daughter in a cage, but that felt a little *too* dark, so I opted not.

Instead, he's got Ikari locked up.
What a gem.

Pazari
The
Merchant
Fox
Fritz
Daughter?
cute?

KHWAM

Khwam was always a massive bear with glowing blue eyes in my head. What   is a better way to embody Despair, than a giant, unmoving beast that doesn't care if you ever leave?

But toward the end of writing, I had a thought..what if he was white? Not that the protagonist would know what a polar bear is, but *we* do, and that makes it even cooler. Get it? Cooler? ...I apologize.

Despair is cold. It freezes you in place. It's the weight that settles over you like a never-ending blizzard.

And suddenly, making Khwam a creature of the cold just clicked. Out of all the embodiments, he's the hardest to fight. Not because he's aggressive, but because he doesn't have to be. He's not chasing you. He's not tricking you. He doesn't want anything from you.

He's just there, waiting to see if you give up first.

Kwan the Bear
Glowing blue eyes
crying

MAP

OF

EVERMOURNE

THE COTTAGE
KWAM'S CAVE
PAZARI'S CART
KYOHI FOREST
IKARI'S CAMPSITE
THE VILLAGE